BACKYARD TENT

Written by Kira Daniel
Illustrated by Ray Burns

Troll Associates

Library of Congress Cataloging in Publication Data

Daniel, Kira.
   Backyard tent.

   Summary: Dan finds that his "just about perfect"
friend Jake does have normal shortcomings when they
sleep out in a tent in Dan's back yard.
   [1. Camping—Fiction. 2. Friendship—Fiction]
I. Burns, Raymond, 1924-   ill.   II. Title.
PZ7.D218Bac   1986   [E]   85-14068
ISBN 0-8167-0626-3 (lib. bdg.)
ISBN 0-8167-0627-1 (pbk.)

BACKYARD TENT

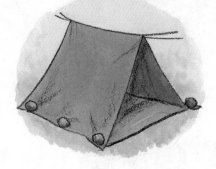

"Tonight's the night," said Dan.
"Tonight Jake sleeps over."
Dan had planned for a week.
He knew tonight would be
special.

"All the kids like Jake," thought
Dan. "Jake is the tallest in the
class. Jake can hit a baseball
farther than anyone else. Jake
can blow huge bubbles with
only one piece of gum. Jake is
just about perfect. Everyone
knows that."

Then Dan sang to himself:

"Jake is tall. He's fast. He's great.
He's coming here.
And I can't wait."

Dan was making a tent. Jake was special. So Dan wanted a special overnight. He and Jake would sleep outside. They would sleep in a tent in Dan's backyard. Dan threw a fuzzy blue blanket over the clothesline.

"What's the tent for?" asked
Lena, Dan's little sister.
She held her teddy bear. She
watched Dan closely.

Dan fixed the blanket. It
flapped in the wind. But soon it
began to look like a real tent.

"Jake is coming over tonight,"
said Dan. "And this is where
we're going to sleep. Someday
you'll be big like Jake and me.
Then you can have a tent, too."
"Oh," said Lena.

Dan put heavy rocks on the
corners of the blue blanket. He
spread an old green blanket on
the grass inside the tent. He
stepped back to look at the new
tent. Lena stepped back, too.
Dan walked around the tent.
So did Lena.

"Looks good," said Lena.
"Good enough for Jake?" asked
Dan.
"Looks *very* good," said Lena.

"I'd better try it out," said Dan.
"Me, too," said Lena.
Dan and Lena crawled into the
tent. Lena left her teddy bear
outside. She didn't want to mess
up Jake's tent.

15

"Sit carefully," warned Dan.
Dan sat down slowly.
Lena sat down slowly.
"I like how the light shines
through the blue walls," said
Dan.
"Me, too," said Lena. "What
will you and Jake do here
tonight?"

"Oh, all the things big kids do," said Dan. "I'll pack the backpack. I'll carry out extra blankets and lots of other stuff, too. Like dinner. Peanut butter and jelly sandwiches, maybe. And tuna sandwiches—my favorite."

"Yum! Mine, too," said Lena.
"After dinner we'll roll out our
sleeping bags," said Dan. "It
will be dark. So we'll need a
flashlight. Jake will tell scary
ghost stories. Then I'll tell scary
ghost stories. We'll stay up *very*
late."

"How late?" asked Lena.
"Past midnight," said Dan.
"Past when the crickets chirp."
"Wow," said Lena. "That's
late!"

"And then," said Dan, "we may go search for wild animals. You know. The ones that come out at night. Like bears."
"No bears live around here!" said Lena.
She smiled.

"I know," said Dan. He liked to
tease his little sister.
"Then what?" asked Lena.

"Then we'll talk," said Dan.
"We'll talk about being friends.
We'll talk about all the things
we can do together. Later we'll
sleep—until the sun comes up.
Then we'll eat breakfast in the
tent. We'll pack up our things—
until Jake sleeps over again."

23

"When is Jake coming?" asked
Lena.
"Soon," said Dan. "Maybe he's
here now. Let's go see."
They wiggled slowly out of the
tent. Lena picked up her teddy
bear. Then they ran to the front
door.

"He's here!" yelled Dan.
"Jake!" yelled Lena.
She hid behind Dan.

Jake was with his mother.
"Hi, Dan," said Jake. Jake held
his sleeping bag.
"Hi, Jake," said Dan. "We're
going to have a great time!"
"I know," said Jake.

He kissed his mother goodbye.
Then he whispered something to
her. Then he kissed her goodbye
again.

"This is my first overnight," said Jake.

"Great!" said Dan. But he was surprised. He had had lots of overnights already. But he didn't tell Jake.

"We're sleeping outside," said Dan.
"Outside?" asked Jake.
"Yes. In a tent," said Dan.
"In a tent?" asked Jake.

Dan showed him the tent.
"I like the tent," said Jake. He
stood up tall. "But do you think
it's safe? Are there bugs in
here?"
Dan laughed.
"Yes, of course it's safe. And of
course there are bugs!" said
Dan.

Dan laughed. Lena laughed.
Jake did not laugh.
Dan picked up his sleeping bag
and his backpack.

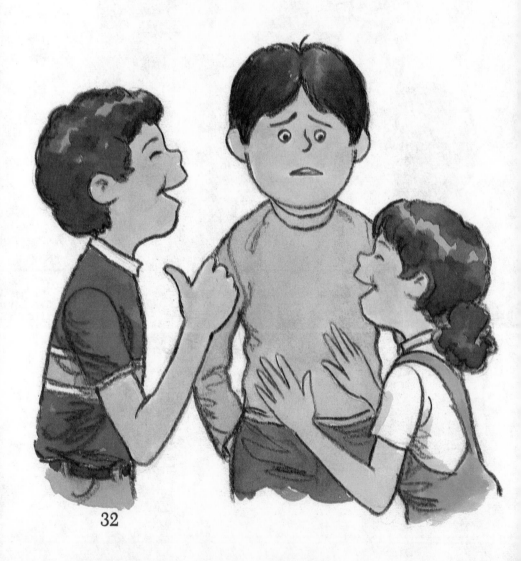

"I've got everything we need,"
said Dan proudly. "Food, extra
blankets, flashlights . . .
everything!"
They waved goodbye to Lena.
And they were off.

They crawled inside the
beautiful blue tent. First Dan
unpacked dinner.

"Do you want a peanut butter
and jelly sandwich or a tuna
sandwich?" asked Dan.
"Yuch! I hate tuna!" said Jake.
"I'll take peanut butter."

"Jake seems different," thought
Dan. But he didn't tell Jake. He
didn't tell him he loved tuna
sandwiches either.

They rolled out their sleeping
bags. It got dark. Crickets
started to chirp. Jake turned on
a flashlight.

"Let's tell ghost stories," said
Dan.
"I don't know any," said Jake.
"Want me to tell you some?"
asked Dan.
"No," said Jake. "Ghost stories
scare me."

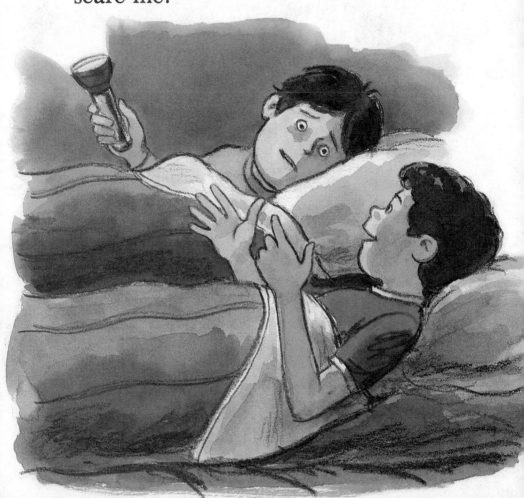

Dan was surprised. But he
didn't tell Jake.

"Want to go out and look for
wild animals?" asked Dan.
Jake sat up straight. "There are
wild animals here? Any bears?"
he asked.

Dan shined his flashlight on
Jake. He looked at his friend.
Jake's sleeping bag was pulled
up over his head. Jake looked a
little scared.
"Don't worry, Jake," said Dan.
"No bears live around here."

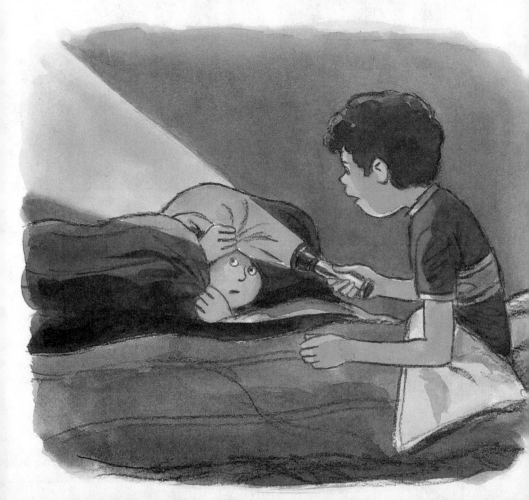

Dan looked at Jake again.
"Want to go into the house?" he
asked. "We could sleep in my
room."
"Great!" said Jake. And he ran
into the house with his sleeping
bag. Dan followed him.

They spread out the sleeping bags in Dan's room. Then Dan turned out the light. They lay in the dark. At first they didn't talk.

"I hope I didn't let you down," said Jake.

"It's okay," said Dan. "I *was* surprised. I was surprised this is your first overnight. I was surprised you don't like bugs. I was surprised that ghost stories scare you. I was surprised you're afraid of the night. I was even surprised that you don't like tuna fish. But you're still my friend, Jake."

"You won't tell anyone. Will
you?" asked Jake.
"Not if you don't want me to,"
said Dan.

"One more thing," said Jake.
"Yes?" asked Dan.
"Could we turn on a night
light?" asked Jake.
Dan smiled. He turned on the
night light.

Jake fell asleep. Then Dan sang
quietly to himself:

"Jake's my friend. Not perfect.
But real. I like him more now.
Yes, that's how I feel!"

48